The Case of the
Secret Tunnel

For Freya
—H.W.

For Hugh and Judy with my love
—M.L.

Text copyright © 2014 by Holly Webb
Illustrations copyright © 2014 by Marion Lindsay

First published in Great Britain in 2014 by Stripes
Publishing, an imprint of Little Tiger Press.

All rights reserved. For information about permission
to reproduce selections from this book, write to
trade.permissions@hmhco.com or to Permissions,
Houghton Mifflin Harcourt Publishing Company, 3 Park
Avenue, 19th Floor, New York, New York 10016.

www.hmhco.com

Text set in Adobe Garamond

*Library of Congress Cataloging-in-Publication Data
is on file.*

ISBN: 978-0-544-81554-4

Manufactured in the United States of America
DOC 10 9 8 7 6 5 4 3 2 1
4500608541

THE MYSTERIES OF
MAISIE HITCHINS

The Case of the

Secret Tunnel

BOOK 5

WITHDRAWN

written by
Holly Webb

illustrated by
Marion Lindsay

Houghton Mifflin Harcourt | Boston New York

31 Albion Street, London

Attic:
Maisie's grandmother and Sally the maid

Third floor:
Miss Lane's rooms

Second floor:
Mr. Grange's rooms

First floor:
Professor Tobin's rooms

Ground floor:
Entrance hall, sitting room, and dining room

Basement:
Maisie's room, kitchen, and yard entrance

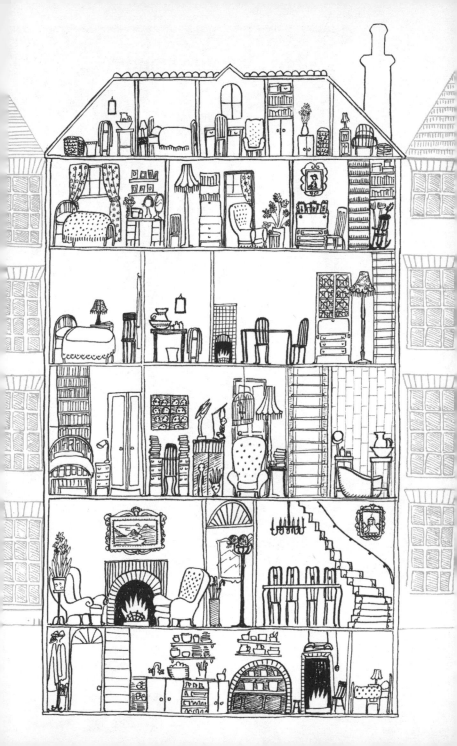

"Is that your new dress to wear for the wedding?" Maisie asked Alice, a little wistfully. They were in Alice's bedroom, and she had just noticed the beautiful lace-trimmed blue silk dress hanging up on the front of Alice's enormous wardrobe.

"Yes!" Alice bounced up and down excitedly in her pink velvet armchair. "I didn't really need it, but Papa said I should look smart for Madame Lorimer's special day. I went to her for French lessons for years, you know. I shall miss her, but I'm looking forward to the wedding. Especially as you'll be there too, Maisie!"

Maisie nodded, but she didn't say anything. The girls had met when Alice had started lessons with Madame Lorimer, who rented a room in Gran's boarding house. Quite often, Madame dozed off in the middle of the lesson, and then Alice could sneak out and gossip with Maisie. Otherwise, the two girls would never have been friends —their lives were simply too different. Alice had French conversation, dancing classes, and deportment, while Maisie learned how to cook and do laundry.

Alice frowned at Maisie. "What's the matter? Aren't you looking forward to the wedding?"

"Yes, of course I am. Especially as Professor Tobin is going to escort me and Gran home afterward on the Underground. I've never been on it before." Maisie folded the skirt of her old purple dress between her fingers. "But I haven't got anything to wear." She looked over at Alice, who stared back at her in surprise.

Maisie held back a sigh. Alice couldn't possibly understand. She always had new dresses, lace-edged petticoats, and handmade boots.

Gran's boarding house was very respectable, but it didn't bring in a lot of money. There certainly wasn't enough for new dresses, even for wearing to a wedding. Madame Lorimer had rented the rooms on the second floor at 31 Albion Street for as long as Maisie could remember, but now that she was getting married she'd be going to live in her husband's big house in Richmond. Gran would have to find a new lodger and, until she did, money would be even tighter than usual.

"I only have this dress," Maisie added, her cheeks flushing pink. She held out her faded skirts and looked sideways at Alice.

Alice nodded thoughtfully. "It's a lovely color," she said, clearly trying to think of something nice to say.

"It was . . ." Maisie muttered.

"Why don't you borrow one of mine!" Alice dashed back over to her wardrobe and flung open the doors.

Maisie caught hold of Eddie by the collar. He was a well-behaved little dog—mostly —but he was even nosier than Maisie was. He just liked investigating things. Interesting

4

cupboards, particularly, in case there was food in them. She could see his ears pricking up already. "No, Eddie. It's only clothes. You can't go and get muddy pawprints on them."

Alice giggled and pulled out the folds of a bright floral summer dress. "You could get muddy pawprints on this one, Eddie. My aunt sent it to me for my birthday, and it's *foul*. But, Maisie, look. *This* dress would be

perfect for a wedding." She lifted out a pretty, pale green silk frock with a flounced skirt and little pearl buttons down the front.

Maisie's eyes widened. She'd never worn
a dress like that.

"It would suit you," Alice said
persuasively. "The color would be so nice
with your red hair, and it would match your
green eyes."

Maisie swallowed and dug her fingernails
into her palms to help her stop imagining
herself in the green silk dress, hobnobbing
with all the grand folk at the wedding party.

"I can't, Alice. It's a beautiful dress. But Gran wouldn't let me borrow it. She . . . she'd say it wasn't proper to go begging dresses off you. I shouldn't have said anything."

"But you didn't beg! I asked if you were excited about the wedding, that was all." Alice frowned. "Would she really mind?"

Maisie nodded. "Gran's very proud, Alice. She'd say it was charity and that we've never had to ask for anyone's help."

Alice looked at her doubtfully, but she pushed the green dress back into the wardrobe and shut the heavy doors—with difficulty, as the wardrobe was full to bursting.

Maisie stared at the pretty rug on the floor, embarrassed. "How's your new governess?" she asked, trying to change the subject.

Alice made a face.

"Miss Darling's not nice?" Maisie asked anxiously. She felt a little bit responsible. Alice's father, Mr. Lacey, knew about Maisie's detective work and had actually employed her to inspect all the applicants for the job of governess. She'd had to pretend to be a maid doing the dusting, so she could spy on the ladies as they waited to be interviewed for the job. In the end, she had told Mr. Lacey that she thought the best of the bunch was Miss Honoria Darling, who had helpfully moved her chair so Maisie could dust the large vase behind her, and had smiled at her very sweetly. All the rest of them had been grumpy. Alice's father had paid Maisie a whole shilling. Now she was worried that she hadn't deserved it.

"She's *too* nice . . ." Alice sighed. "That's the problem. Papa is smitten with her."

"Oh no!" Maisie stared at Alice in horror. "I'm sorry!"

Alice's father was a widower, and Alice definitely didn't want him to get married again. She had read too many books about evil stepmothers, and she didn't want one. So Alice had given Maisie a huge bag of toffees and asked her to look out for any sly governesses who might be angling to marry Mr. Lacey.

"It isn't your fault, Maisie. It isn't her fault, either. She's just . . . lovely. I ought to hate her, but I don't, which just shows, doesn't it?"

Someone tapped lightly on the door, and it started to open.

"That'll be her—shhh!"

"What if she recognizes me?" Maisie squeaked. "It's too late to hide . . ."

Alice jumped up, snatched a brush and a ribbon from her dressing table, and started to fuss with Maisie's hair, pulling it back from her face to make her look different.

"Good afternoon, Miss Darling. This is my friend Maisie."

The new governess stepped into the room and smiled. "Alice has told me all about you!" she said, sounding pleased to see Maisie. Unlike Alice's old governess, Miss Sidebotham, who had always looked as though she thought Maisie smelled. "It was you that found dear Snowflake and her kittens, wasn't it?"

Maisie nodded and watched as Eddie went over and sniffed suspiciously at Miss Darling's shoes. "We had to take Snowflake and the kittens down to the kitchen. They don't get on with Eddie."

"No, I can imagine . . ." Miss Darling stooped down to let the dog sniff her fingers.

"A great big strong fellow like you . . . You couldn't leave a cat unchased, could you?"

Eddie licked at her fingers adoringly, and Maisie stared. He was friendly, but not usually *that* friendly.

"You see! Even Eddie thinks she's wonderful," Alice whispered in her ear. "Miss Darling, Maisie is going to the wedding tomorrow too. That's why I was advising her on how to wear her hair," Alice said, twisting Maisie's hair into a coil at the back of her head. "But she doesn't have a smart dress, and her grandmother won't let her borrow one of mine . . ."

Miss Darling looked at Maisie thoughtfully, and Maisie went red again. It was bad enough that Alice knew she didn't have anything to wear. But Miss Darling nodded and said tactfully, "You're taller than Alice, Maisie. I don't think her frocks would suit you. But what about borrowing a collar? I'm sure your grandmother wouldn't mind that."

"Yes!" Alice jumped up and ran to her chest of drawers. "I have lots of lace collars, Maisie, can't I lend you one of them?"

Maisie frowned. Surely Gran couldn't mind just a collar?

Alice pulled out a pretty one, and Maisie

stroked the lace admiringly. It would make the whole dress look different. Alice held it around her neck and pushed her toward the mirror. "You see! So smart! You simply *have* to take it." And she added in a whisper, "I told you! She's nice, *and* she's clever. I'm doomed . . ."

Chapter Two

"Madame Lorimer looks lovely!" Maisie whispered to Alice. "Even in that horrible hat!"

"I think it's quite a smart hat," Alice said thoughtfully, staring at the mountain of pink and red feathers that Madame Lorimer was wearing.

Of course, they'd have to remember to call her Mrs. Mossley now.

Maisie stared at her friend, and Alice giggled and reached out for another chocolate eclair. "Look at your face, Maisie! You're right, it's like she's got a giant mushroom on her head. But she still looks nice. It's lovely to see her so happy." Alice licked chocolate off her fingers contentedly and nudged Maisie. "Which do you think is bigger? The hat or the cake?"

"Mmmm . . . the cake, but only just," Maisie said. She had seen wedding cakes before, in the windows of fancy bake shops. But never one as big as this. It was covered in flowers and pearls and swirls of icing. Maisie wasn't sure how anyone was going to manage to cut it. She was very glad that Eddie hadn't been invited—she didn't want to imagine what he would do to a cake like that . . .

"I'm really not at all sure about this,
Professor. The Underground . . ." A couple
of hours later, Maisie's grandmother hesitated
outside Richmond Station and clutched her
little box of wedding cake nervously.

Professor Tobin patted Gran's arm
soothingly. "The Metropolitan Underground
Railway has been running for many years
now, Mrs. Hitchins. And the track is
aboveground out here at Richmond. We'll
go into a tunnel part of the way through the
journey, that's all. We shall be at Baker Street
Station before you know it."

"But going down underground, Professor,
with all that earth on top of you! It just
doesn't seem right. And I remember when

they were building it, you know, and the Fleet Sewer burst and flooded it. Who's to say that won't happen again?"

"The tunnels are all closed in now. I'm sure it's safe," the professor promised.

"Oh, I suppose so . . . And it will be quicker than the horse tram. I am quite tired, after the wedding party." Gran sighed doubtfully, but she took a step inside the tiny ticket hall, and Maisie beamed at the professor. She had never been on the Underground either, and she was desperate to see what it was like.

Mr. Mossley had paid for horse-drawn carriages to take his guests out to his Richmond house after the ceremony, but it was up to them to get themselves home. Professor Tobin had suggested they travel back by Underground. He had been quite shocked to hear that Maisie and Gran had never even been into one of the stations.

"Now, we buy our tickets here," he explained, ushering Gran over to the ticket window. "No, no, my treat, Mrs. Hitchins." He jingled through his pockets, searching for change. "There we are, sixpence for all of us, to Baker Street, please, young man."

The railway clerk pushed the little card tickets through the slot, and the professor guided them down the steps to the platform, which was practically deserted in the middle of the afternoon. A very tall man in tattered work clothes was pacing to and fro at the other end of the platform, swinging a grubby tool bag, and there were a couple of smartly dressed ladies sitting on one of the benches, but that was all.

Maisie was glad that Richmond Station

was at ground level — she found the idea of climbing down under the earth rather frightening too. Of course, they would be underground by the time they got to Baker Street, but going up out into the open air seemed less strange.

"Why, it looks just like a normal steam train!" Gran said in surprise as the train creaked to a halt in front of them a few minutes later.

Maisie nodded. She had traveled to the countryside with Alice a few weeks before. This train was almost the same as the one they had taken from Paddington, just a little smaller. She wasn't quite sure what she had expected. Something that looked safer for traveling along tunnels cut deep through the earth? Something with armor-plating, perhaps. The little carriages were

neatly painted, though rather dusty, but they didn't look as though they would be much protection against falling rocks . . .

The professor politely held open the door of an empty compartment in the second-class carriage, and Maisie stepped inside. The velveteen seats were grimy, but there was a gas lamp, flickering on the wall. Maisie gave a little sigh of relief—she had been worried that the journey would be in the dark.

They sat down and Gran clutched Maisie's hand tightly as the engine wheezed and clanked away, clouds of smoke and steam puffing past the windows.

"Where does all that smoke go when we're in the tunnel?" Maisie asked the professor curiously.

He sighed. "Most of it stays in the tunnel, Maisie. There are vents, of course, but even those are a problem. They belch out steam and frighten the horses on the road up above. I must admit, the atmosphere in the tunnels is somewhat thick . . ."

Gran glared at him, her eyes bulging a little. "So now we're to be suffocated? Oh, I knew we should have gone by the horse tram!" Then she let out a little squeal as the train dived into a tunnel, puffing and blowing like an angry troll, and the view of the grassy cutting was swallowed up in darkness.

It's very eerie, Maisie thought as she stared out at the blackness. It was more than just an absence of light—more like a thick black fog swirling around the carriage. Maisie wasn't usually afraid of the dark, but she shuddered as she imagined what might be hiding out there in all that black space beyond the windows.

The gas lamp flickered more than ever and the professor looked worried. He clearly thought that Gran was about to faint. "Here, Mrs. Hitchins, someone has left a newspaper. Perhaps you could read to calm your nerves?"

Gran unfolded the newspaper with

shaking fingers and began to read the front page. Maisie peered over her shoulder—she felt like being distracted too. "Oh! Gilbert Carrington!" she exclaimed, seeing a familiar name leap out at her.

"The detective?" Professor Tobin asked. "Has he solved another case?"

"No . . ." Maisie murmured, skimming the dense print. "No, he's in New York." She sighed. Gilbert Carrington lived on Laurence Road, very close to Maisie's house. In fact, they would walk past his house on their way home from Baker Street Station. He was the most famous detective in the world, and Maisie had studied his methods. She had even seen him in person a couple of times, dashing into a cab outside his house, obviously on the trail of a criminal.

"He's still investigating that murder, you know," Maisie reminded Professor Tobin. "The one with the odd messages left in the tree outside the victim's window. Mr. Carrington solved the code, but the murderer fled to America. All it says here is that he's in New York now and that the police have just consulted him by telegram about a case." She glanced up at the headline. "'Art Thieves Still at Large.' Oh, it's that Sparrow Gang! They've stolen another painting, and in broad daylight again. George, the butcher's boy, told me Charlie Sparrow's seven feet tall, and that he's killed people! Two of his gang double-crossed him, so he chopped them up into bits!"

"Don't listen to errand boys' gossip, Maisie. It says here that the police think the thieves are popping up out of the sewers," Gran said, shuddering. "Disgusting."

"I suppose the sewers do go everywhere," Maisie said thoughtfully. "And the Underground tunnels too," she added as they pulled into a brightly lit station. The walls were papered with colorful advertising posters, and a few more travelers climbed in further down the train.

"Exactly!" Gran snapped. "There are probably all sorts of revolting things leaking into this tunnel from the sewers."

"Not much longer now, dear lady," the professor assured her. "Ah! Baker Street is the next stop," he added. "Gather your things, Mrs. Hitchins. The trains don't wait for very long."

But just then the train plowed to a halt in the middle of the tunnel, with a sharp squeal of brakes.

"I knew it! I knew it!" Gran cried. "There's been a crash. We're doomed!"

Maisie jumped up and lowered the little window, peering cautiously out into the tunnel. She could hear people fussing and calling, so she leaned out and shouted, "Why have we stopped? Has there been an accident?"

"Lady collapsed!" someone called from further up the train. "Fainted dead away, poor dear. We'll be moving shortly. Someone pulled the emergency cord."

"I'm not surprised," Gran said, between coughs. "Shut that window, Maisie! You're letting in all those poisonous fumes!"

Gran was still coughing when they pulled into Baker Street Station a few minutes later. She leaned heavily on Professor Tobin's arm as he led them off the train and over to the lift. Maisie saw the lady who'd fainted on the train being helped by the station staff, who fussed over her while other passengers offered advice. She had a hat that was nearly as huge as Madame Lorimer's.

They stepped into the lift. Maisie squealed as it lurched suddenly upward and her stomach seemed to stay behind. Gran let out a horrified groan and pressed her handkerchief to her face. "It isn't natural," she moaned as she tottered out into the ticket hall. "It shouldn't be allowed." Then she went into another spasm of coughing, so loud that one of the ticket clerks hurried over, looking worried.

"Are you all right, madam?"

"It was the smoke," Maisie explained.

"Oh, you need to go to the pharmacy next door," the man said, nodding helpfully, his fair hair flopping forward over his face.

Maisie blinked, trying to work out where she had seen him before.

"It's Mrs. Hitchins, isn't it? Bert Dodgson. I rent a room with Miss Barnes, next door to you on Albion Street." He smiled at them.

"You need a bottle of Metropolitan

Mixture, Mrs. Hitchins. Specially made, it is, for those overtaken by the fumes."

"You see?" Gran muttered to Professor Tobin as they slowly climbed the stairs out to the street. "It's unhealthy, this Underground business. Why else would they be making special medicines for it?"

Maisie looked back down the steps and sighed. It had been a gloriously scary adventure and she couldn't imagine when she would next have the chance to travel on the railway.

"But an artist, Gran! That would be much more interesting!" Maisie pleaded, looking up from scrubbing the kitchen table.

Gran folded her arms grimly and shook her head. "Artists don't pay, Maisie. Poor as churchmice, all of them. No, I want a nice, clean, sensible lodger. Who do you think would be cleaning up after a painter, Maisie Hitchins?"

Maisie sighed. She had liked the artist. He had a pointed beard and he'd managed to get streaks of blue paint down one side of his hair. Gran had also refused to rent the rooms to a violinist, a friend of Miss Lottie Lane, the actress who lived on the top floor. He played in the orchestra at the theater where Miss Lane was appearing and he'd seemed quite respectable. But Gran had told Maisie afterward that she just couldn't abide the noise. It was like a cat being strangled. She hadn't said that to the musician, of course—she'd told him that Professor Tobin suffered from terrible headaches and had to have a quiet house.

"A nice-sounding young man is coming to see the rooms this afternoon," Gran told Maisie now. "He came to ask about the rooms this morning, but he was on his way to work and in a bit of a hurry, so he'll be back later for a proper look. I just hope he's suitable. I don't want those rooms standing empty for any longer than they have to."

Maisie wrinkled her nose. *Nice* sounded rather boring. "What does he do?" she asked.

"He works as a clerk in the office of a biscuit company," Gran told her.

Eddie looked up at Gran hopefully. He liked the sound of this young man too.

"Very quiet," Gran went on. "Lovely manners. No nonsense, not like some I could mention."

Between Miss Lane coming home from the theater at midnight and Professor Tobin filling his rooms with stuffed animals and strange tribal masks, Gran was sick of interesting lodgers. But Maisie thought that working in a biscuit factory sounded desperately dull.

"Perhaps he'll bring home samples," she said, trying to look on the bright side.

Chapter Three

Mr. Fred Grange *was* dull. He was polite, clean, and utterly boring, which meant that Gran thought he was the perfect lodger. He liked the rooms, which Maisie felt he certainly should, considering how long she and Sally the maid had spent cleaning them. So Mr. Grange moved in that very afternoon, with nothing but a couple of carpetbags. This made Maisie's gran like him even more. It had taken her ages to recover from Professor Tobin arriving with a cartload of packing cases, assorted weapons, and a shrieking parrot.

Gran sent Maisie up to take Mr. Grange some tea. As Maisie looked around the second-floor rooms, she couldn't help missing Madame Lorimer. Until only a few days ago, there had been lacy tablecloths everywhere, and vases of wax flowers that were awful to dust. But now the rooms looked quite empty. Mr. Grange didn't seem to have many personal belongings at all. Not even a picture of his mother, or a sweetheart. And no biscuits, either, Maisie noticed sadly.

"Thank you . . . Maisie, is it?" He took the tea and began to usher her toward the door, almost as though he wanted to get rid of

her, Maisie thought. "I'll bring the tray down later."

"Would you like me to help with the unpacking at all?" she asked, but he shook

his head firmly and shooed her out, shutting the door behind her with a determined click.

Maisie stood on the other side of the door, feeling rather cross. She had only wanted to help! And perhaps to nose about a little, but that wasn't anything to be ashamed of. It was important that she and Gran knew a bit about the lodgers. They knew next to nothing about this one.

Over the next few days, Maisie didn't learn a great deal more. Mr. Grange left for his work early in the morning and didn't return until nearly dinnertime, so he was obviously very hardworking. He hated kippers, he'd told Gran, when she asked about meals. Then so did anyone with any sense, Maisie thought.

But after Mr. Grange had been at Albion

Street for a few days, Maisie made a surprising discovery. She had gone out to buy some groceries for Gran and was hurrying back with her basket when she saw Mr. Grange. He was nowhere near his offices, which were several streets away, at the back of the biscuit factory. He was standing at the door of a tall, shabby-looking house, talking in whispers with a tall, shabby-looking man. A suspicious man, Maisie thought at once, as she noted the hat pulled down low over his face, and the way he kept glancing from side to side, as though he were keeping watch on the street.

Maisie sucked in an excited breath. She didn't want their new lodger to be up to no good—of course she didn't—but this did make him a great deal more interesting . . .

She walked past quickly, hoping that

neither of them had noticed her watching

them. She didn't want to put Mr. Grange on

his guard.

After that, Maisie kept a much closer eye

on the new lodger. Instead of Mr. Grange

being desperately boring, she began to think

of him as mysterious. For example, on a

perfectly dry Monday afternoon, how could he come back from work with his boots so plastered in mud that Maisie had to scrub the tiled hallway? He was apologetic about it, at least, when he came back down the stairs and found her on her knees with a bucket of hot water and a scrubbing brush. He'd changed his boots, thank goodness, so he wasn't still tracking mud everywhere.

"Oh! I'm sorry, Maisie. I didn't notice I'd brought in all that mud. Um, here . . ." He fished in his jacket pocket and passed her a penny. "I must have trodden in a puddle," he added rather vaguely.

But there *were* no puddles on his way to work, Maisie reflected, putting the coin in her apron pocket. She knew that because she had been to the factory a couple of days earlier, after she'd spotted him loitering in the street. She hadn't been quite sure what she was expecting to find out, but she knew it was something that Gilbert Carrington would have done. She had even copied down the sign outside the factory in her notebook — *Libbey's Fine Biscuits and Crackers. Made with the purest of ingredients.*

Maisie carefully examined the mud too, as she cleaned the floor. But it just looked like mud, even through the magnifying glass that the professor had given her.

Despite the lack of useful clues, Maisie was sure there was a lot more to the new lodger than first appeared. In fact, she was wondering if he really worked at the biscuit factory at all. It was time to test him out, she decided, as she sluiced the muddy water down the drain in the yard.

"Maisie, bring the washing in, since you're

out there!" Gran called from the kitchen. "It must be dry by now in this wind."

Maisie wiped her damp hands on her apron and went to unpeg the washing—mostly the professor's, although there were some of Miss Lane's pretty underclothes as well. She stacked the washing in the baskets that had been left by the door and carried them in to Gran, who was heating the irons over the stove. Washing took up most of Monday, as Gran and Sally and Maisie did it all themselves to save money, rather than sending it out to a laundrywoman. There were odd bits of washing done in the rest of the week too, but most of it was saved up for Mondays.

"Good gracious! Where did this old-fashioned thing come from?" Gran exclaimed, as she turned over the washing

in the first basket and held up a wide
petticoat made of grayish-white woolen
flannel, stained with mud around the hem.
"That's not Miss Lane's—she wouldn't be
seen in something so scruffy!"

Maisie frowned. "It was on the line, Gran.
Is it Sally's?"

Sally popped her head around the door from the scullery and snorted disgustedly. "It most certainly is not! Miss Lane wouldn't wear it and neither would I!"

"But where's it come from then?" Maisie asked.

"And more to the point, where are the professor's combinations?" Gran snapped. "Maisie, is this some sort of silly joke?"

"No! Honestly, Gran, I just brought in what was on the line. Maybe I left them . . ." Maisie hurried out into the yard again, but the washing line was empty—the professor's droopy woolen underclothes were nowhere to be seen. She looked around the yard, biting her lip. Gran would be furious if she couldn't find them. What would she tell the professor? And why on earth would someone steal woolen underclothes anyway?

Maisie stood by the washing line, scowling. Could someone have pulled them off the line by accident? One of the delivery boys, perhaps? Then she gave a triumphant gasp— there was a scrap of white trailing out from behind the outhouse. Maisie darted over and snatched up the muddy combinations. Gran wouldn't be pleased about having to wash them again.

"But what on earth happened?" Gran muttered when Maisie told her where she'd found the muddy underwear. "It makes no sense . . . If it hadn't been for the petticoat you found, I'd have thought you'd just dropped them, Maisie." She darted a stern look at her granddaughter, but then patted her hand. "However careless you are, you do tell the truth. Except when you're messing around with that detective nonsense.

Humph!" She snorted. "Well, here's a mystery for you, Maisie. It's a pity your Mr. Gilbert Carrington's in New York, isn't it? The Case of the Droopy Drawers . . ."

"That's odd . . . It isn't only your clothes going missing, you know," George said to Maisie in the yard the next morning. She had asked him about the washing when he'd brought the meat delivery. "Next door had something nicked off their line as well. Last Monday it would have been, I suppose. Miss Barnes had the cheek to say it was me what took it! And I didn't, before you ask, Maisie. What would I want with her unmentionables?"

"It must be boys playing tricks . . ." Maisie said doubtfully. "I don't mean you,

George," she added, as he glared at her. "Gran said I should try and solve the mystery, but it has to be someone being stupid. What else could it be?" She frowned to herself. It was interesting that it wasn't only their washing that had been messed about with, though. She wondered if anyone else on the street had been affected. Maybe it *was* a real mystery after all . . .

"Did Miss Barnes find anything on her washing line that wasn't meant to be there?" Maisie asked George, but he only scowled.

"How do *I* know? I was too busy running away. She nearly boxed my ears!"

"Maybe I'll ask up and down the street," Maisie murmured. "You never know." Missing washing might not be as exciting as missing paintings, but it was worth investigating.

The newspapers were still full of stories about the infamous Sparrow Gang and their string of art thefts. There had been another painting taken, just a few days before, from a grand house in Richmond. In fact, it had been the very same day that Maisie had been in the neighborhood for Madame Lorimer's wedding.

The article she had read that morning said the police were baffled, particularly as the thefts were being carried out in broad daylight. One of the paintings had turned up in France, offered for sale to a private collector, who had recognized it and informed the French police. So Charlie Sparrow, the leader of the gang, had obviously managed to smuggle it out of the country. The article suggested that was probably what had happened to all the others. They were somewhere in Europe, sold to collectors who knew quite well that they were stolen.

How annoying to have been in Richmond, so close to the scene of the crime, and not to know anything about it, Maisie thought, as she took the meat delivery in to Gran. She might even have seen the thief!

Still, I've got my own detective work to do, Maisie told herself. She would ask around about the washing, and she mustn't forget to try to find out some more about Mr. Grange and his muddy boots and suspicious friends.

She got her chance that afternoon when she met him coming in from work. She eyed his boots, but they were reasonably clean. His coat was damp, though, Maisie noticed, as he lifted his hat to her in the hallway. How could that be? It had only rained in the middle of the afternoon — Gran had sent her running out to bring in the professor's newly washed combinations off the line, so Maisie knew it had. But surely a clerk would have been at work in his office at that time, not out getting wet?

"Mr. Grange!" she called, as he started up the stairs.

He turned, looking back down at her, and Maisie sighed silently to herself. He was so very normal-looking, with his mousy hair and plain sort of face. He didn't look at all suspicious now.

"Would you like some tea and biscuits?"
Maisie asked, thinking quickly. "You look
chilled, sir. I bought some Garibaldi biscuits
this morning. Very nice with tea. Or cocoa,
perhaps?"

"Oh—oh, that's kind of you, Maisie, but
I'm quite all right. I'm not really partial to

Garibaldi biscuits—I don't like coconut."
And Mr. Grange hurried up the stairs to his
room, leaving Maisie staring after him, open-
mouthed.

It had worked far better than she could
have expected. She had only been trying
to get him to talk about biscuits, so she
could ask about his job—just to be on the
safe side, really. Mr. Grange had looked so
pleasant, and so, well, boring as he crossed
the hallway. It had seemed foolish to suspect
that there was something going on. She
hadn't expected him to give himself away.

But someone who actually worked in
a biscuit factory would know all about
biscuits. He'd know that Garibaldi biscuits
had currants, and not even a hint of coconut.

He *was* lying, after all!

"Is it convenient for me to sweep your floor, sir?" Maisie asked, hovering hopefully outside Mr. Grange's door a few minutes later and trying to peer inside. If she could only get into his room, she was sure that she'd be able to take a closer look and find out what he was really up to. "I noticed when I dusted this morning that I hadn't quite got all the mud from yesterday out of the cracks in the floorboards."

"Oh, er, not at the moment, thank you," Mr. Grange murmured. "Perhaps later. I'm working just now."

"On biscuits?" Maisie said, catching a glimpse of a pile of papers on the table.

"I beg your pardon?"

"You're working on biscuits?" Maisie nodded at the papers, and then suddenly realized how nosy she sounded. She smiled at him. "I do love biscuits. You're ever so lucky, working at a biscuit factory. But don't you find that you're hungry all the time? With the smell of baking?"

"Oh! Er, yes . . ." Mr. Grange nodded.

"What's your favorite kind of biscuit? I like shortbread, myself." She knew she sounded completely wooly-headed, but it didn't matter. In fact, if Mr. Grange thought she was just a silly girl, he was less likely to worry about clearing away his papers. "And Marie biscuits," she added, beaming at him.

"Ah! Well, um . . . digestives. I like digestives. I must get back to work now, Maisie. I'll be going out shortly—perhaps you could sweep up then?"

Maisie nodded. "I'll be back later."

Digestives. Really. The most boring biscuits of all were his favorite? Maisie was more and more convinced that Mr. Fred Grange knew nothing about biscuits at all.

When she heard the front door bang a little while later, Maisie bundled the potatoes she'd been peeling into a pan and snatched up the broom. "Gran, I'm just going to sweep Mr. Grange's rooms—he was working earlier and didn't want me to disturb him."

"But you swept all the rooms this morning, Maisie!" Gran turned around from the stove, looking confused.

"I didn't get all that mud up properly!" Maisie darted out of the kitchen, clutching the broom, with Eddie trotting after her.

As Maisie had hoped, Mr. Grange had left his work on the desk. Maisie had obviously convinced him that she was stupid. It was a little insulting that he had believed her so easily, Maisie thought, but she wasn't going to complain. She hurried over to the table and stared down at the sheet of paper lying there.

It was a list, Maisie saw at once. But a strange one—not a shopping list, or a list of things to remember. And certainly nothing to do with biscuits.

Maisie stared at it, unconsciously trailing her fingers over the spiky letters as she read. This was a list of paintings—familiar ones, too. It was a list of the paintings that had been stolen by the Sparrow Gang. He was adding up how much they were worth.

Malton Venus £600??

Lady Anne Letherby £450??

Cupid and Psyche £500??

Brancaster Wedding Portrait £500??

Sir John Leighton and a horse £750??

Her heart thudded so hard, and so quickly, that she felt sick. One of the Sparrow Gang was lodging in Gran's second-floor rooms! She'd been bringing him his meals and fetching him cups of tea! She had cleaned a master criminal's muddy boots!

There was a fumbling sound at the door, and Maisie whirled round. She had been concentrating so hard on the list, she hadn't heard the footsteps on the stairs. Taken completely by surprise, she stood like a statue by the table, staring at Mr. Grange, who was framed in the open doorway.

Chapter Four

It seemed that Mr. Grange was just as shocked as she was. He froze in the doorway, gaping at her.

Maisie grabbed the broom again. She thought it might be good to have a weapon, just in case. She fixed on her silly smile and swept the broom busily across the floor.

"Did you forget something, Mr. Grange, sir? You only just went out."

"You were reading those papers," he said coldly, shutting the door behind him and coming to stand over her. She hadn't realized quite how tall he was until now. Eddie let out a low growl and tried to push himself in between Maisie and Mr. Grange. But he was only a very little dog.

"I was dusting the desk, sir, that's all." Maisie tried to sound natural, but her voice wobbled. He knew quite well what she'd been up to. And what would a master art thief do to someone he caught nosing about in his papers?

"Do you know what it is, that list you · were reading?"

Maisie tried to back away, but Mr. Grange caught her arm and she panicked. There was no point pretending that she didn't know who he was. "It's a list of paintings!" she shouted, and Eddie barked angrily. "Paintings you stole! You're a thief—you're Charlie Sparrow, or one of his men. And if you don't let go of me, I'll scream! There'll be a police officer here in seconds. Seconds!"

Fred Grange — or Charlie Sparrow — let go of her at once, his mouth falling open in surprise, and Maisie scuttled back against the wall, getting as far away from him as she could. Eddie darted from her to the lodger and back again, growling and whining.

Why is Mr. Grange looking so shocked, Maisie wondered. He must have realized she'd worked out he was part of the gang, or why would he threaten her like that?

Then, infuriatingly, he began to laugh, his plain, boring face going scarlet as he laughed so hard, he struggled to breathe.

Maisie scowled at him. "I *will* call a police officer," she said angrily. "I don't care if you think it's funny. Where have you put all those paintings? Where are they?"

The man stopped laughing and gazed down at her grimly. "I only wish I knew."

"Have you lost them?" Maisie nibbled her bottom lip. He wasn't behaving like a criminal. Had she made a mistake?

"What makes you think I'm Charlie Sparrow?" He flung himself down into an armchair and looked thoughtfully at Maisie. Eddie sniffed at his trouser legs, and the lodger leaned down and stroked the little dog. He suddenly didn't look quite so threatening . . .

But he had definitely lied. Maisie folded her arms and glared back at him. "You've got a list of the stolen paintings. You were adding up how much you'd get for them."

"And that's your proof? What were you doing snooping around in here anyway?" he demanded.

Maisie sniffed. "You lied to Gran. And me. You said you worked for Libbey's Biscuits, and you don't."

"How on earth do you know that?" The lodger sat up straighter in the armchair, frowning.

"You don't know what a Garibaldi biscuit is. And you said *digestives* were your favorite."

"I do like digestives," he told her. "So you were trying to catch me out, were you? Wittering on about biscuits like that?"

Maisie nodded. "I saw you hanging about with a suspicious character, and then you were covered in mud when you shouldn't have been. And when you came home this afternoon, your coat was soaked through. People who work in offices don't need to go out in the rain in the middle of the afternoon, Mr. Grange—if that's really your name, which I don't believe for a minute." She eyed him, noting the way he was sprawled in the armchair. He really didn't look like an art thief who was about to be reported to the police. "Although maybe you aren't Charlie Sparrow, either," she admitted reluctantly. "But you're definitely a liar, and probably a criminal, and I shall tell Gran so! She'll give you your rent back and ask you to leave. She only chose you because you were—" Maisie hesitated.

"What?"

"Boring," she told him, with a shrug. "Gran thought so anyway. Boring and quiet, and she thought you'd pay the rent on time."

"I will," the lodger said quickly, sitting up again and staring at her. "I will, Maisie, I promise. Look, you can't tell your grandmother. I need this room. And I'm not part of the Sparrow Gang, or any sort of criminal at all."

"You're not still trying to tell me your

name's Fred Grange and you really do work for Libbey's Biscuits," Maisie said with a sigh.

"Not quite . . . Fred Grange is my real name, that part's true. But you're right, I don't know a thing about biscuits." He  glanced up at her again and sighed, obviously deciding to trust her. "I'm a policeman. Detective Constable Grange."

Maisie gave a disbelieving snort, but he nodded at her.

"Go and find a police officer, if you like. They'll vouch for me. But do it quietly, Maisie. Don't make it too obvious."

Maisie narrowed her eyes. "Are you

undercover then? You're not very good at it, are you?" That wasn't much of a surprise, to be honest. The police investigating her previous case, the theft of Professor Tobin's rare feathered mask, had been completely useless, she thought. But that had actually been quite lucky, since it had turned out that the professor knew the thief—a boy called Daniel. Once they had discovered what was going on, the professor and Maisie had conspired to help Daniel escape back to South America right under the noses of the police.

"What, because I didn't know enough about biscuits?" Fred shrugged. "Yes, I admit it. I should have made sure there weren't any holes in my cover story. But it all had to be done in a bit of a rush. We'd heard there was a room going spare on Albion Street, you see."

"What, so it's not just by chance that you're lodging in our house?" Maisie came closer, her eyes widening. "Why here?"

Fred chewed his lip, but then he obviously decided he didn't have a lot of choice. Maisie already knew so much that he had to trust her. "Because of who you've got living next door, lodging with Miss Barnes. Charlie Sparrow's little brother."

Maisie gaped at him. "Really? But Miss Barnes, she's so respectable!" She giggled. "Oh, I wish I could tell Gran." Maisie's grandmother and Miss Barnes had been keeping up a polite rivalry for years. Gran would be very smug if Miss Barnes turned out to have been harboring a dangerous criminal.

"You can't tell anyone!" Fred snapped, and Maisie just stopped herself from rolling her eyes. She knew that!

"I won't." She looked at him thoughtfully. "But in return, you have to tell me what's going on."

"What?" Fred shook his head fiercely. "You're a little girl!"

Maisie did roll her eyes this time. "A little girl who spotted you," she pointed out. "So . . ."—she plumped herself down on the rug in front of the hearth—"tell me about this brother. I must know him," she added, frowning, "if he lives next door. But I don't think there's a Mr. Sparrow . . ."

Fred nodded, rather reluctantly. "They're half brothers. Bert Dodgson, he's called."

Maisie gasped. "But he's nice, Mr. Dodgson! He works at Baker Street Station, selling tickets. We saw him just the other day—he was worried about Gran when the smoke made her cough."

Fred shrugged. "He's definitely Charlie's brother. But you're right, he doesn't look suspicious. He's never been in trouble—or not much, anyway. He's never been caught, let's put it that way. He's respectable. And he's why I'm here. We're sure he must know something about what his brother's doing, even if he isn't actually part of the gang. So it's my job to watch him. To look out for anything strange going on in the house next door. Odd visitors. Bert popping out and about at strange times. You see?"

She nodded, fascinated. An undercover policeman, in her house! Even if he wasn't a very good undercover policeman, it was still exciting. Particularly as it was perfectly clear to Maisie that Fred Grange was going to need her help . . .

Chapter Five

"Sorry, Maisie!" Fred Grange raced down the stairs, struggling into his jacket as he went, and Maisie flattened herself against the wall.

"Whatever's the matter?" she gasped. "Are you going out? You haven't had breakfast!"

"Another picture gone!" he hissed. "Early this morning, just reported. I've been called to a meeting at the Yard."

New Scotland Yard . . . the home of the detective branch. Maisie sighed as the front door banged behind him. At least she was planning to do her own detecting today too. Gran was still cross about the washing, and she'd told Maisie at supper the night before that she'd spoken to one of their neighbors while she was waiting to be served at the butcher's. The same thing had happened to Mrs. Ferrars a couple of weeks earlier—washing taken, and a man's old nightshirt left in its place. It must be going on up and down the street.

Maisie had decided to go and talk to Miss Barnes next door, and ask her exactly what had happened. From what George said, Miss Barnes had been furious when the washing was taken, so maybe she wouldn't mind Maisie doing a little bit of sniffing around. And, of course, if she happened to catch a glimpse of Bert Dodgson at the same time, she wouldn't complain.

After she'd finished washing up the lodgers' breakfast things, Maisie nipped out into the alleyway behind the backyard and went in through the neatly painted wooden door to number 29. Miss Barnes was in the yard, hanging out some washing, and she spun around at once, glaring at Maisie fiercely.

"Oh, it's you, Maisie! I thought it might be one of those dratted boys again."

"The ones who've been messing about with the washing lines?" Maisie asked sympathetically.

"You heard about it, did you?" Miss Barnes nodded grimly.

"I came to ask you about it—the same thing happened to us."

"It's getting beyond a joke. The first time it happened I thought I was mistaken. That I'd mixed up the laundry, perhaps. But then it happened again."

"Oh, I didn't know it had happened twice," Maisie said, surprised.

"Twice?" Miss Barnes snapped. "Five times, Maisie! Our nice things taken, and then those scruffy horrible garments hung on the line in their place. I've reported it to the police, even! And it was most embarrassing, describing exactly what had been taken." She lowered her voice to a ladylike whisper. "Petticoats, and . . . drawers. I swear that young officer was sniggering behind his notebook, and no one's done a thing about it."

"They took the professor's combinations off our line. But they left them behind the outhouse." *Why has Miss Barnes had so much washing taken?* Maisie wondered. Perhaps it was because she was grumpy and always scolding children for shouting in the street. Was someone trying to get revenge? "They left an old flannel petticoat instead," Maisie added.

"Humph. Would you like another one to go with it?" Miss Barnes gestured at a pile of garments in the corner of her yard. "I wouldn't give houseroom to any of them. I'm waiting until the ragman comes round."

Maisie went over to look. "This has all been left on your line, then?" she asked, crouching down to turn over the faded heap —two grubby shirts, and three red flannel petticoats, all flounced and embroidered in a very old-fashioned pattern. "They're all red. Well, reddish . . . That's odd."

Miss Barnes sniffed. "I suppose it is."

"Maybe it's part of some game," Maisie suggested. "Always to put red things on the lines. But the petticoat on our washing line was white."

"Game! If I ever catch any of them, I shall drag them down to the police station by their ears."

"I'll come and tell you if I find anything out, Miss Barnes," Maisie promised.

She walked back along the alleyway, wondering about that pile of red clothes. Where had they come from? It seemed a lot of effort to go to for a silly game. If it was local lads—or girls—messing about, wouldn't they just swap the washing around between the different lines in all the yards?

The way someone had been putting red clothes on Miss Barnes's line made it seem more important than a game, somehow. More as if it meant something. Maisie paused with her hand on the gate latch, thinking of Gilbert Carrington, and the murderer's coded messages that had sent him running off to New York. Maybe the red clothes were like a code too, or a signal.

Later that morning, Maisie happened to look out of the back window, over the yard. She was polishing Professor Tobin's furniture, and she had noticed that his rooms smelled stuffy and too much of parrot. She was fighting with the stiff sash window, trying to pull it up, when she saw it. The washing flapping about in next door's yard.

She was too bothered with the stupid window to notice it at first, but then a few seconds later the window slid up with a sudden lurch and Maisie realized what she had seen. Someone taking washing off the line! Someone in a dark jacket—a man's jacket, so not Miss Barnes or her maid, Rosa. Stealthily, she leaned further out the window, trying to see who it was. But he was hidden behind Miss Barnes's flapping washing . . .

A sudden screech from Jasper made

Maisie jump and nearly hit her head on the underside of the window.

The parrot made the man in next door's yard jump too. He turned around and looked up toward the noise. Maisie gulped. She shook her apron out of the window as though it was dirty, pretending that dusting it off was all she'd been doing, and then turned away.

"Shhh, you dratted bird, you gave me a fright," she called back into the room.

She waved her feather duster around, and hummed a little tune to herself, rather shakily, acting as though she hadn't been looking at the yard at all. Out of the corner of her eye, she saw the man stop staring up at the window and quickly pin something red onto the washing line, then dart away out of the back gate.

It was Bert Dodgson.

Maisie hurtled down the stairs and into the kitchen, with Eddie scurrying after her. Luckily, Gran was snoozing by the stove, and Sally was on her afternoon off, visiting her mother and little sister. No one would notice that she'd gone to follow Bert from next door—not for a while, anyway.

The problem was, Bert *would* notice her.

She had recognized him at the station, and he'd have seen her around Albion Street. If he was part of the gang, he would be keeping a careful eye out and he'd spot her following him. Maisie muttered crossly to herself, looking around the kitchen for something she could use as a disguise. Curly red hair was not ideal for a detective. It was far too conspicuous.

She didn't have time for anything elaborate. Maisie pulled off her boots and stockings and stuffed them into the broom cupboard. Then she snatched Gran's old shawl from the hook behind the door. Gran only used it when she had to nip out into the yard, and it was raggedy and fraying. Maisie wrapped it around her head to hide her distinctive hair and hurried out into the yard, bending down to dip her hand in the dust, then smearing a dark streak across her face. Now if someone glanced at her they'd see a scruffy little waif, too poor to afford boots or a coat.

"Try to look hungry!" she muttered to Eddie. "Actually, don't worry, you always do."

She edged out of the gate into the alleyway and hurried down to the larger road at the end, wondering how far ahead Bert Dodgson was. It had only taken her a minute or so to grab her disguise, but he could be a couple of streets away by now, lost in the city. She was sure that the strange behavior with the washing must mean something. Maybe he was part of the Sparrow Gang, however well he had hidden it up until now. And now she might have missed her chance to see him meeting with the rest of the gang! She couldn't go very fast to catch up with him, either—she wasn't used to not wearing shoes, so her feet were soft and delicate compared to those of a real street child. She had to step carefully.

But Maisie was lucky. As she slunk down the street, trying to look inconspicuous, she saw Bert coming out of a tobacconist's shop, not far ahead of her. She and Eddie fell in step behind him as he set off down the street.

It only took Maisie a couple of corners to work out where Bert was going—and she sighed. Of course—Baker Street Station. All her dreams of finding Charlie Sparrow, and perhaps even the stolen paintings, slipped away. Bert was just going to work. Now that she got close, she could even see that he was wearing his dark uniform suit, with the brass buttons.

She watched as he entered the station, and then turned away with a sigh. "That was useless," she muttered to Eddie as they plodded back the way they'd come.

Eddie whined sympathetically. He was used to Maisie talking to him, and even though he didn't understand what she was saying, he could tell that she wasn't happy.

"You're a very good and faithful assistant," Maisie murmured, leaning down to rub his flyaway ear. "I wish we'd found something useful just now. Mr. Grange thinks I'm a silly little girl who's getting in his way. And I don't think we're going to change his mind by telling him that Bert Dodgson likes messing about with washing lines." She frowned. "But that must mean something, mustn't it? It can't just be that he likes annoying old ladies. I know lodging with Miss Barnes must be horrible, but would he really go around stealing clothes to get back at her?" Maisie sighed. "If that's what he's doing, then maybe he isn't part of the gang. He wouldn't put them all at risk to do something so silly."

Then she stopped, so suddenly that Eddie kept going for a few steps until he realized she wasn't with him anymore. "It isn't *silly!*" Maisie whispered. "Eddie, it's not silly at all!

What if it *is* like Gilbert Carrington's case? The red clothes *are* a message! But what do they mean?" Maisie frowned to herself as she opened the gate to the yard behind number 31. She was sure she was on the track of the mystery at last, but she couldn't quite pin down how everything fit together.

She had been out for only about a quarter of an hour, and Gran was still dozing when Maisie walked into the kitchen and hung up the shawl. She quickly washed her feet—in freezing cold water, though (she couldn't risk waking Gran by heating it on the stove)—before putting her stockings and boots back on.

Then she sat at the kitchen table with her little notebook open in front of her, trying to work out what was going on. Eddie flopped down lovingly over her feet.

"If Bert's signaling with the red clothes, perhaps it's to tell someone else that a painting's been taken . . ." Maisie whispered, scribbling *Red signal* in her book. "Or perhaps it's to say 'danger'? What does white mean, though? And why has he put five signals on Miss Barnes's line and only one on other people's? It's as if they aren't as important. Oh!" Maisie dropped her pencil and it went rolling off across the table.

Gran snorted and shifted in her chair, and then drifted back off to sleep with a ladylike snore.

"The other people aren't important, Eddie! I bet they don't mean anything. It's a cover, that's all!" Maisie thumped her fist lightly on the tabletop. "There's been a red signal five times, for five paintings . . . And now a sixth time, this afternoon—the very same day that Mr. Grange went racing off to New Scotland Yard, because there's been another theft! If I went back and asked Miss Barnes, I'm sure I'd find out that every time someone messed with her washing line, it happened just after a painting got stolen. Bert Dodgson's signaling to the rest of the gang, trying to tell them something about the paintings. That's why he puts red clothes on the line—because red's easy to see."

Maisie laid down her pencil, grinning triumphantly. "But if he only used Miss Barnes's line, she might get suspicious. So he steals things up and down the whole street, to cover up that it's only one washing line that really matters!"

Chapter Six

Maisie couldn't wait for Mr. Grange to
get back so she could tell him what she'd
worked out. But he stayed away till late in
the afternoon—obviously busy investigating
the latest theft by the Sparrow Gang.

"I'm sure it would be useful to know
about the gang's signals," Maisie said to
Eddie as she carried Miss Lane's tea tray
downstairs. "Maybe whoever Bert's signaling

to lives close by! Someone else in the gang. They could do a search . . . Perhaps I should have gone to New Scotland Yard and asked for Mr. Grange. But he's undercover—I don't want to get him into trouble. Oh!" She squeaked joyfully as she heard a key turn in the front door. She dumped the tray on the side table in the hall next to a china vase.

Fred Grange came in, looking tired. "Hello, Maisie," he muttered. He sounded dispirited, as though the investigation was not going well. "I may not be here much longer—I'd better warn your grandmother. The chief inspector thinks watching Bert Dodgson is a wild goose chase, as he's never gone anywhere near any of the scenes of the crime. Maybe it's not even the Sparrow Gang stealing the paintings. Who knows? Not us, certainly . . ."

"Bert Dodgson *is* part of the gang, and he doesn't need to go near the scenes of the crime," Maisie said, catching Fred's sleeve as he made wearily for the stairs. Eddie danced excitedly around his feet.

"What?" He turned and blinked at her.

"What are you talking about? Look, could you fetch me a bowl of hot water, please? I need to wash."

"Bert Dodgson is signaling to the rest of the gang using the washing line in the back yard of 29 Albion Street," Maisie told him. She was trying to sound calm and sensible, but she couldn't help a gleeful note creeping into her voice. She had uncovered an important clue!

"What? Is this what your grandmother was complaining about? Someone stealing washing? I thought it was the local children."

"That's what the gang *wanted* everyone to think!" Maisie explained. "But there have been six painting thefts, including one this morning. And then I saw Bert Dodgson putting a red flannel petticoat on next door's washing line this afternoon! It's already happened five times, always with red clothes. The white things on the other lines are just a red herring." Maisie giggled at her accidental joke, then hastily straightened her face, trying to look serious. "He's sending messages, I'm certain of it. You said the police were sure that Bert must be involved, and he is."

Mr. Grange was looking at her very thoughtfully. "This all sounds a bit far-fetched, Maisie, but if you definitely saw him messing about with the washing line . . ."

"I did!"

"Perhaps I'd better get back to the Yard and tell them," Mr. Grange said.

Maisie sighed. "I really didn't want him to be a thief. He was so nice when we saw him at the Underground station. And I don't understand why he works there, either," she added. "It can't be for the money, can it, if he's part of the Sparrow Gang?"

Mr. Grange was pulling his coat on hurriedly. "As a cover, I suppose. Tell your grandmother I won't be in for dinner."

"It would be a good place to hide things, down there in the dark," Maisie said suddenly, as Mr. Grange made for the door.

Slowly, he turned to stare at her, his eyes wide and appalled. "In the Underground tunnels? Why didn't we think of that?" he murmured. "We've been going about this all the wrong way. I must go back to the Yard! There's no time to lose, especially now, with the duke coming to London."

"What duke?" Maisie frowned.

"Haven't you heard? I thought you read your grandmother's newspaper. Duke Leopold, the German prince? He's some sort of cousin to the queen, though she has so many cousins, I wonder she can remember them all. He's coming to London to hold a show of his paintings — great treasures, some of them. Hundreds of years old. The queen will come and visit. The chief inspector is terrified. I swear to you, Maisie, his hair's gone two shades grayer since he heard the duke was coming. We can't let the Sparrow Gang get near those paintings, but we don't know how to stop them. Charlie Sparrow seems to be a master of disguise. He sneaks in, somehow, and the paintings simply disappear."

"Can't they tell the duke not to come?" Maisie suggested.

"What, tell him that the whole of the London police force can't protect him and his paintings? We'd look like fools!"

Maisie couldn't help thinking that would be better than looking like fools *after* the duke's paintings had been stolen, but Mr. Grange obviously didn't agree.

"It would cause a diplomatic incident," the policeman muttered. "It just can't happen. I must get back to the Yard and tell them about the signals, and the Underground tunnels."

"Can I come with you?" she started to say, but Mr. Grange was gone, banging the door behind him before she'd even finished her sentence. She was left standing alone in the hall with Eddie and a tray of dirty tea things.

"It isn't fair, Eddie," Maisie murmured as she dried the china. "*I* worked it out! I bet he won't even mention me when he tells his inspector all that new evidence!"

Eddie looked up at her over the huge marrow bone that he'd dug up from the corner of the yard.

"And here I am, washing up! I should be tracking the gang, not them. It isn't fair!"

"Life isn't, Maisie," Gran told her, as she hurried by from the larder. "Now, have you finished that drying up yet?"

"Nearly." Maisie sighed. She supposed it was better not to be chasing down Charlie Sparrow. George had said he was fearsome and huge, and had killed at least two men who'd double-crossed him. But it was so frustrating to be stuck at home, not even knowing how the police investigation was going.

"Good. Go and take that dog for a run and blow the cobwebs away. You're so cross, your hair's practically sticking out sideways. And I don't want to know what the matter is, Maisie! I know quite well I shan't like it."

Gran usually turned a blind eye to Maisie's detecting. She didn't really approve, because she thought it was unladylike to be so nosy. But she'd had to admit that it could be useful sometimes.

"Thanks, Gran!" Maisie pulled off her apron and reached up to give Gran a kiss, before she snatched her shawl and darted out into the yard. It was a chilly day for March—she'd noticed that earlier on when she'd followed Bert—and it was getting dark now. The yard was full of shadows thrown by the strange half-light of dusk, and she kept Eddie close as she marched along the street. Gran had been right to send her out, even though it was getting dark. She had been stewing over the unfairness of it all, and the brisk, chill air was helping to calm her down.

"One day," she muttered to Eddie as they reached the gates of Regent's Park and she turned for home again. "One day, I shall be a proper detective, like Gilbert Carrington. And the police will come and consult *me* for help. Not run off and do all the interesting parts of the investigation on their own."

Eddie trotted along next to her, snuffling happily through piles of rubbish and sniffing at fascinating lampposts.

"We should practice," Maisie told him. "Look, there's a man up ahead of us—we'll track him, hmm? We'll try following without anyone noticing us. We were lucky with Bert Dodgson earlier on—we'd have lost him if he hadn't come out of the tobacconist's at just the right time. Tracking is an essential skill for a detective—and I don't have your nose, Eddie."

Maisie felt herself walking differently as soon as she decided that she was detecting. Her shoulders tightened and her head went forward—just like Eddie's did when he was on an interesting scent. "Stop it," she said to herself, forcing her feet into a slower, more natural sort of walk. If she caught up with the man, he'd look around and notice her, and the whole point was to track him without being spotted.

She glanced at the figure up ahead, trying
to memorize what the man looked like.
Dark jacket. Dark trousers. Boots that looked
like anybody else's boots. He had a cap on,
rather shapeless and battered, so he wasn't a
grand gentleman. He didn't have a walking
stick, either, or a neatly folded umbrella
against the rain that was just starting to

fall. Just an everyday sort of person, then, walking along, whistling a tune. Maisie grinned, stopping herself from humming along with him. Miss Lane had taught her that song, "Ta-ra-ra Boom-de-ay"!

The only interesting thing about the man was his hair, which coiled out from under the cap in curls that were almost as springy as Maisie's, though a lot darker. The curls shone as he went under a street lamp. Perhaps he was wearing hair oil. But other than that he was really quite boring.

"Doesn't matter," Maisie whispered. "I should think most criminals look just like everybody else." She wasn't going to be able to follow him for much longer. She would have to go home soon. But luckily the man seemed to be heading in much the same direction as Maisie. She kept waiting for him to turn off a different way, but it was as though he was going all the way to Albion Street.

He was in Glentworth Street now, the road that ran parallel. Maisie hurried after him, suddenly more interested, and gave a gasp as he turned determinedly down the narrow side road that led to the alley along the back of Albion Street. It was an odd little road, and it didn't even have a proper name. Gran called it Albion End, but there was no sign up on the wall. Maisie always thought the road might have been a mistake. It didn't really go anywhere, but against the wall halfway down was an old stone drinking fountain. It looked as though people had expected the road to be busy, once upon a time.

It was getting darker now, but Maisie hung back as the man hurried around the corner into Albion End. It was likely there'd be no one else in the narrow little road, and she didn't want him hearing her footsteps. As she got to the turning she peered cautiously around, wondering if he was far enough ahead for it to be safe to follow him.

But he wasn't there.

Maisie stood at the end of the road, her secretive pose forgotten, and simply gaped. Where had he gone? There were no gates opening into the alley. Had he realized she was following him and sped up into a run as soon as he'd turned the corner? But Albion End was paved. She would have heard his running footsteps on the stones. Especially since she'd looked quite carefully at his perfectly normal boots—they didn't have rubber soles for quietness. She would have spotted those.

So how on earth had he disappeared so quickly?

And more to the point, why?

Chapter Seven

"You look peaky, Maisie. Overtired. Here
you are." Gran set a steaming mug of cocoa
down in front of her. "Not that it tastes the
same, of course. I can't get used to this new
kind—I told Mr. Jessop in the grocer's so.
It isn't nearly as good. I still can't see why
Bartram's went out of business—theirs was
quite the best cocoa. And this new one is
tuppence more a tin!"

Maisie sipped carefully at the hot cocoa. "It's still nice, Gran. Thanks."

But the cocoa didn't make it any easier for Maisie to sleep that night. She couldn't stop thinking about the man in Albion End —the way he had disappeared. And then there was the Sparrow Gang. She had hoped to stay up until Mr. Grange came back, so he would tell her what was happening. She wanted to know what the police were doing with the evidence she had found. But Gran made her go to bed straight after she'd finished her drink.

Fred Grange had come back eventually, very late, as Gran had pointed out disapprovingly the next morning. Then, as Maisie was wearily setting out the professor's breakfast tray, Mr. Grange popped his head round the kitchen door.

"No breakfast today, thanks. I've got to get over to the . . . er, the factory. Got an emergency on!"

"A biscuit emergency?" Maisie muttered, scowling at him. Couldn't he see she wanted to ask him about the case? But he was already gone. She thumped the professor's plate of eggs and bacon down on the tray.

Gran glared at her. "Careful, Maisie! Are you feeling ill?"

"No, Gran." Maisie tried to smile brightly. She didn't want to be forced to take cod liver oil. It was disgusting, and Gran swore by it for any sort of sickness.

"What's the matter?" Professor Tobin asked as she set his breakfast down on the little table in his room—next to a stuffed dormouse and some strands of seaweed.

"How do you know something's the matter?" Maisie asked, surprised.

"You're not the only detective in the house," the professor joked. "You haven't said a word, Maisie. And look at Eddie's face—he can tell there's something wrong as well."

"Oh . . ." Maisie sighed. "I can't tell you —I promised. There's a case, you see, and I helped, but it isn't really mine to investigate. The police are involved. And now I don't know what's happening. No one's telling me anything!"

"Ridiculous," the professor said, his huge eyebrows drawing together as he frowned. "The police. Useless lot. But this all sounds most interesting, Maisie. Couldn't you keep investigating by yourself? Or did you promise not to?"

Maisie looked at him thoughtfully and smiled. "No . . . actually, no, no one said I couldn't. That's a very good point, sir. Thank you!"

"Just be careful," Professor Tobin said. "Don't take any silly risks. And I want to know all about it when you're done."

Maisie went back downstairs to eat her own breakfast, wondering what would be the best thing to do. She didn't want to get in the way of the police investigation, of course she didn't. But surely she could do something useful? Something that it would be hard for policemen to do?

She nibbled at her toast, frowning to herself and feeding Eddie crusts under the table. Fred Grange was truly terrible at being undercover; she had proved that. And the police were busy trying to guard the duke's paintings. So perhaps she could help out, watching the main suspect. Maisie was sure it must be important that Bert Dodgson worked at the Underground—all those tunnels were perfect for hiding things. And Baker Street Station was a public place—no one could complain if she visited it. She probably wouldn't see anything, but at least it would feel like she was still part of the case. And she might be able to spot one of the gang . . .

Maisie hurried through her work, hoping to slip away in the afternoon, but Gran kept finding errands for her, and it was after supper before she got the chance.

"What are you up to?" Sally asked her, laughing, as Maisie whisked the dishes away.

"Are you wanting to go and visit Alice?" Gran asked.

"I haven't seen her for days," Maisie said, crossing her fingers in the folds of her apron and telling herself that detectives had to bend the truth sometimes. She didn't like lying to Gran, but she hadn't actually said she was going to see Alice . . .

"Oh, go on, then. But don't be back too late!"

"I won't!"

Maisie fetched her shawl and a covered basket. She had a feeling that dogs might

not be all that welcome on the Underground
— not scruffy little dogs, anyway. She might
need to hide Eddie away. And the basket
was useful too, she thought, slipping a
woolen scarf and an old hat of Sally's into it,
just in case she needed a disguise.

Maisie entered the station cautiously,
keeping an eye out for Bert Dodgson. She
wasn't sure exactly what his hours were.
She wanted him to be there, of course — so
she could watch him and hopefully spot
something important. But she didn't want
to have to buy a ticket from him in case he
recognized her.

Luckily, there were two ticket windows,
and lots of people were milling around the
booking hall, all heading home from work,
Maisie supposed, or perhaps they were out
for the evening. She was able to buy her ticket

—third class, for a penny—from the other
ticket clerk. Bert Dodgson was at the second
window, helping an old gentleman work out
what ticket he needed, and Maisie was fairly
sure he hadn't seen her. She loitered in the
ticket hall, watching him patiently deal with
the old man, who now seemed to have lost
his coin purse and was patting distractedly at

his pockets. Perhaps Bert Dodgson was just too nice to be a criminal?

Maisie nibbled her bottom lip, hoping she hadn't sent the police off on a wild goose chase. The crowd in the booking hall was thinning out—she was going to have to go down to the platforms, or Bert Dodgson would see her. She took the stairs this time, thinking that Eddie might not like the lift. The ticket clerk hadn't mentioned that dogs weren't allowed on the Underground, so she let him stay out of the basket. It would only make him grumpy to be shut up.

Down on the platform there were benches set into the brick walls, with posters stuck behind them. The station was well lit, with great glass lamps hanging from the ceiling—there weren't any shadowy corners to lurk in, but the platform seemed quite busy. Maisie walked along it as far as she could and sat down on a bench. How long would she be able to sit here without someone noticing? She could say that she was feeling ill, she supposed, if anyone asked why she wasn't going anywhere. She'd just explain that she wanted to sit and rest for a while. When they had traveled back

from Richmond, the lady who had fainted on the train had sat on one of the benches, with the guard fanning her with a newspaper and other passengers crowding around, offering advice and smelling salts.

Maisie got out her handkerchief and held it up to her face, trying to look as though she might feel faint. But most people on

the platform were chatting to each other, or peering impatiently into the tunnel, looking for the next train. No one seemed to be looking at her.

And then, of course, when the train arrived, they all crowded on. Maisie smiled at her own foolishness. There was no one left to notice that she was still there! There were passengers waiting on the opposite platform, but their train would be along soon too, whisking them away.

It was only the railway staff that she needed to worry about now. There was a man in uniform on the other side, but he seemed to be busy shooing passengers away from the edge of the platform and answering questions about when the next train would come. If he crossed over and questioned her, Maisie would move on and disguise herself with the scarf and hat before he came back. But several trains puffed in and out of the station and no one came to ask why she was still there.

There was no one sneaking around looking like an art thief, either. Maisie yawned and peered down the platform into the dark mouth of the tunnel. Would anyone really hide stolen paintings in the Underground? It was all starting to seem rather unlikely.

Eddie dozed under the bench, and Maisie felt her own eyes closing too.

Maisie woke up with a jump. Someone had shouted quite loudly right next to her. She'd been caught!

But it was only a gentleman in a silk

hat, complaining about the trains. "Really, this is ridiculous! I've been here fifteen minutes already. The delays on this line are shameful!"

There was a man in the railway uniform on the platform now too, apologizing to the annoyed passengers. Maisie huddled back into the corner of the wall, hoping he hadn't noticed how long she'd been there. It was nearly ten o'clock at night, she realized, peering in horror at the huge clock hanging above the platform. How had she gotten away with sitting here so long? The platform must have been busy all evening. Gran would be frantic, Maisie thought, hurriedly stretching her cramped limbs. She'd have to explain what she'd been doing. Gran would never believe she'd been at Alice's all this time.

"Yes, there's been a delay—someone

taken ill on the train. It'll be here soon — so sorry, sir." The attendant from the railway was threading his way along the platform, muttering apologies. "Ah, here we are."

The train steamed into the station, and the passengers surged toward the carriages. But the attendant shooed them away from the first compartment, opening the door to escort out a couple of ladies, one of whom had obviously been taken ill on the train. She was drooping, and the attendant was half holding her up as she went to sit on one of the benches.

Maisie looked at her curiously as she and Eddie walked up the platform. She wondered how often people fainted on the train. That huge hat couldn't have helped, she thought to herself. It looked so heavy.

Maisie stopped with a jolt, and then

forced herself to walk on by. She knew that hat—with the thick veil, and the puff of purple feathers, and the long trailing ribbons—the lady who'd fainted on the train last time had been wearing the same hat!

In fact, she was fairly sure it was the same lady. The same person who had stopped the train before . . .

Maisie knew she ought to go home. Gran would be worrying about her. But she couldn't leave now! This was another clue! She crept on down to the other end of the long platform and huddled back into the corner of a bench, watching as the woman got up at last and made for the stairs. Should she follow her? Or wait?

The lady in the hat had stopped the train again. That was the important thing. She had pulled the communication cord, but it must have been for a reason—so that something else could happen. Maisie didn't know what, but if she waited, maybe she'd find out.

The platforms were emptying now and the station would soon be closing. Maisie nibbled her thumbnail anxiously, watching a tall man pasting up advertising posters farther along the platform. She'd have to leave when the last train came in, just before eleven o'clock—the attendants would check that no one was left behind, and anyway, she didn't want to be shut in all night. What was it that had happened when the train stopped in the tunnel? Maisie thought furiously, but she couldn't work it out.

Even the man sticking up the posters was leaving now, she noticed. He bounced up the stairs with his tin of paste, going four steps at a time. His legs were enormously long, Maisie thought, getting up to follow him. Whatever had happened, she had missed it, and she'd better get home to Gran.

Maisie picked up Eddie, cuddling him
up against her shawl—he seemed as sleepy
as she was. She yawned as she went past
the new posters, which showed a little boy
smiling as he held up a steaming mug, and
then sighed. She knew that little boy—he
was on the tin too. The posters were for

Gran's favorite, Bartram's Creamy Cocoa. Oh, Gran was going to be so cross with her!

Maisie had gotten to the bottom of the steps when she turned back, nearly bumping into the lady who was following her.

"Sorry!" she murmured, hurrying back to stare at the poster, to check. She hadn't just imagined it . . .

Bartram's Creamy Cocoa had gone out of business. Mr. Jessop the grocer had told Gran so. So why had that man been putting up posters for something that wasn't made anymore?

It was another signal. It had to be! Just as strange as the red clothes on the washing lines. Maisie stared at the little boy on the poster in bewilderment. What on earth did it mean?

"I'll just go down and check no one's fallen asleep on the platform," someone called from the top of the stairs, and Maisie looked around wildly. She couldn't go yet! She hadn't worked out what was going on. What if there was a painting hidden somewhere? This could solve the whole case! She had to stay!

With a nervous little gulp, she darted back along the platform and crouched down, tucking herself underneath the nearest wooden bench. It was a tight squeeze, but she fit, just about. "Shhh, Eddie," she murmured, and he peered at her, confused.

The man came all the way down the stairs and walked along the platform. Maisie peeked out as he passed her and saw, with a funny little lurch inside her stomach, that it was Bert Dodgson.

He was looking for something, hurrying along the platform, gazing up at the walls.

Maisie felt her stomach skip again—she was right! He was looking for the posters!

When he came to the space where the man had pasted up the cocoa poster, Bert Dodgson thumped his fist into his other hand and muttered something. Maisie couldn't hear what, but it was easy to see that he was very pleased. He walked briskly past her, and she knew exactly where he was going.

Back to Albion Street, to put another signal on the washing line.

Chapter Eight

It was all very well being a great detective
and solving the case, or at any rate almost
solving it, Maisie thought. But she was still
locked up in Baker Street Station with no
way to get out. And no idea where a stolen
painting might be hidden, either.

Most of the lights were out now. Just the
odd one here and there was still flickering,
for the sake of the night watchman, she

supposed. He had come down once, with a lantern, and she had ducked back under the bench again. Then afterward she had crept back up the steps to make sure he was safely out of the way. She had seen him, sitting in a little cubbyhole by the ticket office, snoring away. But down here on the platform, she and Eddie were all alone.

"I still don't understand how everything fits together," Maisie murmured to Eddie, huddling him against her to keep them both warm as she stared up at the cocoa posters again. It was chilly down here in the middle of the night. And spooky. She kept hearing rustling noises and rumbles, and what sounded like trains in the distance —except it couldn't be, because all the trains had stopped now. "There are so many different bits. The washing lines. And the posters. And that lady fainting on the train . . . She's mixed up in it too, I'm sure she is. But I don't see why she was doing it . . . Why would anybody *want* to pull the communication cord?" Maisie blinked. People were always collapsing on the Underground because of the fumes. So no one would think it was that unusual. But when the communication cord was pulled, it stopped the train, so the guard could go and find out what was wrong.

BARTRAM'S CREAMY COCOA

"She wanted to stop the train . . ." Maisie murmured, turning around to look back into the dark tunnel. "So someone could get off . . ."

Perhaps a person who needed to get into the tunnel without being noticed—a person with something to hide.

Maisie nodded slowly. She had worked it out, she was almost sure. Charlie Sparrow stole the paintings, hid them somehow, then just walked to the nearest Underground station. The lady in the big hat made sure she got onto the same train, and then shortly before they arrived at Baker Street, she would pretend to faint and someone would pull the communication cord and stop the train. There would be a minute or two before it started again, just long enough for Charlie to slip out. He hid the painting somewhere in the tunnel, and then took some of their stash of posters and pasted it up for his brother Bert to spot. And Bert went home and signaled to . . . to someone else that Maisie hadn't seen yet. Whoever sold the paintings, maybe?

Maisie frowned. If she was right, then Charlie Sparrow must have been on that same train from Richmond that she and Gran had traveled on. Otherwise there'd have been no point in the lady fainting. Her eyes widened as she remembered the tall workman she had seen on the platform at Richmond Station. Had his grubby tool bag been large enough to hide a painting, rolled up?

Maisie gulped. She had been down here a good while since the station closed and Bert went home. Someone could have seen Bert's signal already. They could be coming to pick up the painting now.

So it was up to her to get it first.

She froze as a slow, wheezing grunt
sounded from the tunnel. Another train! But
the trains had finished running for the night.
No one was here to catch a train . . . Maisie
definitely didn't believe in ghosts, but down
here in the cold half-light, it was hard to
remember that . . . She pressed herself back
against the bench as the noise of the wheels
grew louder, clanking slowly into the station.
Ghostly wreaths of grayish steam floated out
around her as the train puffed by. Maisie peered
from behind her hands, wondering who would
be in the carriages, staring out at her.

But there weren't any carriages—Maisie
let out a shaky breath and shook her head as
the train rumbled by. A goods train—with
trucks, covered in tarpaulins. Of course. The
goods trains must use the tunnels at night,

when the lines weren't busy. She watched the trucks disappear into the tunnel, and stood up determinedly. She was going to have to follow the train into the tunnel to find the painting. It must be hidden in there somewhere.

Maisie walked down the platform and peered into the tunnel as the dim lights of the goods train faded away into the blackness. Then she marched back along the platform to the steps, crossing her fingers. The night watchman had looked quite cozy and comfortable napping in his chair. He wouldn't need the lantern if he was asleep, would he? And she was definitely going to need a light—it was blacker than night in the tunnel. It was borrowing, not stealing.

She stopped at the top of the stairs, and smiled to herself. The night watchman was

still snoring loudly and the lantern was
sitting there, just by his chair.

"Stay, Eddie," she murmured, patting his
bottom to make him sit by the top step.
"Shhh." Then she tiptoed out through the
dimly lit ticket hall and waited, holding
her breath, eyeing the lantern. The night
watchman let out a rattling snore and Maisie
seized her chance, grabbing the lantern

under the cover of the noise and scuttling away in triumph.

It was only when she got back down to the platform again that her stomach twisted and the excitement faded away. Now that she had the lantern, there was no excuse not to head into the tunnel.

Maisie crouched at the end of the platform, looking for a way to climb down into the tunnel. She could just about manage to jump onto the track, she thought, but not with Eddie and the lantern to carry. And besides, she wanted to know how to get back up again.

She shivered as she spotted the rickety-looking iron ladder, fixed into the stone under the platform edge. Without stopping to think about it too carefully, Maisie tucked

Eddie into her basket and wriggled around, reaching down with her foot to find the first rung. It wobbled, but she gritted her teeth, and scrambled down until she was standing on the track, dwarfed by the huge opening of the tunnel in front of her. The light of her lantern didn't seem to go very far into the darkness, and Eddie peered out of the basket and whimpered.

"I know it's scary," she whispered. "But I'm sure the painting's here. Somewhere. And if we could get it back, or even just find where they hide them—then the police would have a chance of breaking up the gang, wouldn't they? Detectives have to be fearless, Eddie. Or at least, almost fearless," she added, being honest. She closed her eyes for a moment and took a step into the tunnel, and then she opened them again. "Don't be stupid, Maisie Hitchins," she told herself. "You're no use as a detective if you trip over the rails because you've got your eyes closed. It's just dark." And she marched on, holding the lantern up high and looking for hidey-holes.

"The hiding place must be a little way into the tunnel," she murmured to Eddie. It felt better to talk aloud, even though her voice echoed horribly in the arched shape of the tunnel. "Because the train stopped just outside the station. And it has to be big enough for the posters as well, I suppose. And some pots of paste."

Just then, Eddie let out another whimper, and Maisie gasped.

There was a swinging light coming toward them!

Maisie flattened herself against the wall of the tunnel and hastily wrapped her thick woolen shawl around the lantern. It could only be one of the gang, come to pick up the painting. She could hear his footsteps clumping along the track. He wasn't being particularly quiet—he thought no one would be around to hear. He was whistling to himself, even! The tune bounced along in Maisie's head, and she bit her lip. She wanted to join in, just like last time. *Ta-ra-ra Boom-de-ay! Ta-ra-ra Boom-de-ay!*

It was the man who'd disappeared on Albion End.

She could see his dark curls now, as he lifted up his lantern to look into a niche in the wall of the tunnel, and his whistling broke off mid-phrase. "Ah . . . look at you, you little beauty . . ." He'd propped

his lantern in the niche and unrolled the blanket-wrapped canvas that had been stashed there in a workman's tool bag. He gloated over it for a moment before slipping it carefully back inside. Then he set off down the tunnel again.

It took Maisie only a second to decide — she had to follow him.

The man strode off and Maisie waited, her heart thumping. She couldn't let him get too far ahead, though — she might lose him if he turned off into a different tunnel. And then she'd be lost as well, she thought with a shudder. After a few seconds, she picked her way along the tunnel after him, following as closely as she dared, and trying to mask her footsteps in his own heavy footfalls.

Every time the man stopped, Maisie stopped too, freezing against the tunnel wall and wondering if he'd heard her. Was he going to turn around, hold up his lantern, and catch her huddling there?

But he kept on walking, until at last he paused and reached up for something on the wall. Maisie hung back, pressed against the bricks, hoping that Eddie wouldn't suddenly decide to bark and give her away.

With a last look around, the man began to climb up the wall, as nimbly as a monkey. Maisie stared, and then she realized that there was another ladder, metal rungs set into the bricks, like the ladder she had climbed down to the track. This was his way out. He was about to escape with the painting!

Cautiously, she crept closer, uncovering just a little of her light and peering up. She watched his boots disappear into a shadowy hole at the top of the ladder and held her breath, hoping that he wouldn't close some sort of trapdoor and shut her inside. But all she heard was heaving and scuffling, and then footsteps on paving slabs.

"I bet I know where this goes," Maisie breathed, hooking the basket over her arm and reaching for the ladder. "Now keep still, Eddie. Bet you anything we come out somewhere on Albion End."

Eddie crouched in the basket, looking worriedly over the edge as it swung around. Maisie was trying to keep it still, but it was tricky with the lantern to hold as well, and trying to be quiet. She had to be quick, too —she didn't want to lose the man in the streets above.

The metal rungs creaked and wobbled under her boots as she climbed, and Eddie was starting to whine, but at last Maisie felt the fresh air blowing around her face. She was out! It was still very dark, of course, but there was a lamp lit somewhere up the road. Out here the darkness didn't seem to be wrapped around Maisie like a choking blanket, the way it had underground.

"The fountain," Maisie whispered, as she clambered up. "We're behind the fountain on Albion End. That's how he disappeared!" She crouched behind the stonework and peeped around it, wondering which way the man had gone.

Eddie scrambled out of the basket, shaking his ears in relief. And then, suddenly, he yelped.

Maisie gasped as the darkness thickened again and a figure leaned over her. Just as the man reached down to grab her arm, Eddie snapped at his trouser leg, throwing

him off balance and giving Maisie time to dart away.

"Eddie, run!" Maisie cried.

Her one thought was to get to the safety of home. The man had spotted her. Had he heard her climbing up after him, perhaps? He must have been lying in wait for her behind the fountain . . .

Maisie and Eddie raced down Albion End, toward the alley at the back of their house. Maisie was gasping for breath and she could hear the man thundering behind her. What if he followed her all the way home? What about Gran and Sally? It was the middle of the night, so hopefully Fred would be in his room. That is, if he hadn't stayed away all night at the Yard again . . .

There was a grunt behind her and she felt fingers snatch at her shawl. Maisie dragged herself away, stumbling and flinging herself around the corner and into the alley. She was almost there!

But it was dark, and she had dropped the lantern while she was running, and the latch on the back gate at number 31 was so stiff . . . Maisie fumbled with it, her fingers stupid with fright and her breath heaving so much that she couldn't call out.

"Got you!" the man snarled behind her, and Maisie shoved hard at the door. It gave under her hand, but before she could dart into the backyard, a huge hand covered her mouth.

"Nosy little kid, what were you doing down there in the tunnels, eh?" He didn't take his hand off her mouth to let her answer, though. "Well, you're not going to tell anyone what you saw, missy. Come on."

Eddie barked madly as Maisie kicked

and struggled and tried to break free. But the man was holding her too tightly and he began to pull her back down the alley.

Then, suddenly, there was a light spilling out of the kitchen door, and a great stamping and shouting in the yard.

The man holding Maisie cursed and tried to drop her and run away, but Eddie was darting out of the yard again to snap at the man's trousers. Following him was Fred, and the professor, and a whole host of angry policemen.

Maisie clung on to the man's arm, trying to weigh him down, and Mr. Grange seized him around the neck.

The professor stood in the alleyway with a most deadly-looking revolver, snarling, "One step and I shoot!" And the man stood still, cursing furiously, while Mr. Grange snapped handcuffs around his wrists.

"Of course I reported you missing, Maisie!"
Gran said crossly, handing her a mug of
cocoa. The policemen had finally left, and
they were gathered in the kitchen, eager
to hear more about the gang. "Well, not
officially. But when Mr. Grange got home,
Sally and the professor and I were in a
proper state, worrying about where you'd got
to. I told Mr. Grange that you'd disappeared,
and I thought the poor man was going to
faint. He admitted he was a policeman, and
he told me you might have gone off after
this Sparrow Gang."

"See, he wasn't as boring as he looked,"
Maisie put in, but Gran wasn't listening.

"He sent for reinforcements at once.
All those policemen in my kitchen! I was

shocked, Maisie! Though not as shocked as Miss Barnes will be, of course, when I tell her about her lodger . . ." Gran's mouth twisted at the corner in a tiny smile, but then she looked serious again. "Anyway, Maisie Hitchins, you're a silly, irresponsible, badly behaved little girl. And you're not leaving this house until I don't know when! I've never been so worried! What would I say to your father in my next letter? 'Oh yes, I let Maisie run off hunting art thieves, and she seems to have disappeared'? How could you?"

"But she did catch one of the gang red-handed," Professor Tobin pointed out.

"*He* caught *her!*" Gran exclaimed, slapping a plate of sandwiches down on the table. "If it hadn't been for you, Professor, hearing Eddie barking and dashing out into

the yard like that, we might never have seen
her again!"

"Let's not think about that," the professor
said hurriedly. "Hopefully he'll turn in the

rest of the gang, now they've got him under lock and key."

"Maisie ought to get a reward," Sally said.

"She ought to be sent to bed with no supper," Gran snapped. "And here I am using up a whole jar of fish paste, instead. Just don't you ever do anything like that again, Maisie."

Maisie nodded, but she was smiling into her cocoa. She could tell from Gran's voice that, actually, she was rather proud of her detective granddaughter.

"You shouldn't have done it, Maisie!" Alice said, sounding almost as cross as Gran. She set down her teacup on the little table in

Maisie's bedroom with a clatter and reached for a biscuit. "It was terribly dangerous! Papa and I were very worried when your grandmother came asking after you last night. I had no idea where you were! But I suppose it was very exciting," she admitted, with a little sigh. "So who was he, that man who chased you? Do you know yet?"

Maisie nodded. "Mr. Grange told me about it this morning. At the Yard," she added. She couldn't help smiling as she said it. It had been so exciting, going down there with Gran, almost as though she were a real detective. "He's called Henry Logan. The police were sure he was dealing in stolen paintings, but they couldn't prove anything until now. Charlie Sparrow stole the paintings, hid them in the tunnel, and signaled to Bert with the posters. And then Bert signaled to

Henry with the washing lines. Henry's got a rented room on Glentworth Street, with a view of next door's backyard. It was perfect for spotting the signals."

"And the lady with the big hat?" Alice frowned.

"She's Charlie Sparrow's wife, Peggy. She was wearing that same hat when they arrested her. They've got the whole Sparrow Gang now," Maisie said proudly. "And they think they'll be able to get the paintings back too. Henry Logan had a little book in his waistcoat pocket, with the names of all the buyers."

"Well, I hope you're going to get a reward," Alice said. "Seeing as you were the one who solved the case."

Maisie sighed. "I don't think I will. But Mr. Grange said he was very grateful. After

he'd finished telling me off for putting myself in danger, that is. He's going to be made an inspector." She giggled. "And he sent me this enormous tin of Libbey's Biscuits. I think that's my reward."

"That's not fair!" Alice said.

"I don't mind." Maisie rubbed Eddie's ears, and he gave her chin a sloppy lick. "I still know it was me that caught the Sparrow Gang. Maybe one day I can write my memoirs, and everyone else will know too."

Book One

The Case of the Stolen Sixpence

When Maisie rescues an abandoned puppy, he quickly leads her to her first case. George, the butcher's boy, has been sacked for stealing, but Maisie's sure he's innocent. It's time for Maisie to put her detective skills to the test as she follows the trail of the missing money . . .

The Case of the
Vanishing Emerald

When star of the stage Lila Massey comes to
visit, Maisie senses a mystery. Lila is distraught
—her fiancé has given her a priceless
emerald necklace, and now it's gone missing.
Maisie sets out to investigate, but nothing is
what it seems in the theatrical world of make-
believe . . .

Book Three

The Case of the Phantom Cat

Maisie has been invited to the country as a companion for her best friend, Alice. But as soon as the girls arrive, they are warned that the manor house they're staying in is haunted. With Alice terrified by the strange goings-on, it's up to Maisie to prove there's no such thing as ghosts . . .

The Case of the
Feathered Mask

Maisie loves to look at the amazing objects
her friend Professor Tobin has collected on
his travels around the world. But when a
thief steals a rare and valuable wooden mask,
leaving only a feather behind, Maisie realizes
she has a new mystery on her hands . . .

Find out more about Holly Webb